THIS BOOK BELONGS TO:

_____

_____

_____

meomi

WOULD LIKE TO DEDICATE THIS BOOK TO
ALL OUR FRIENDS WHO ALWAYS KNOW
HOW TO CHEER US UP & ON

Copyright © 2008 Meomi Design Inc. : Vicki Wong & Michael C. Murphy
First hardcover edition published 2008.

immedium

Immedium, Inc., P.O. Box 31846, San Francisco, CA 94131 www.immedium.com

This book was typeset with Rosewood, Usherwood, and hand-drawn Meomi alphabet.
Most of the illustrations were created with the assistance of cute critters with bushy tails.

Edited by Don Menn and Tracy Swedlow
Design by Meomi and Stefanie Liang Chung

Printed in Malaysia. Tenth printing: October 2020.
10

Library of Congress Cataloging-in-Publication Data

Meomi (Firm)
  The Octonauts & the frown fish / by Meomi. -- 1st hardcover ed.
     p. cm.
  Summary: When the Octonauts, a team of eight animal underwater explorers,
meet a frowning fish, they try their best to make it smile.
    ISBN 978-1-59702-014-5 (hardcover)
    [1. Underwater exploration--Fiction. 2. Animals--Fiction. 3. Sadness--Fiction.]
I. Title.
  PZ7.M5322Ob 2008
  [E]--dc22
                                                2008010555

Rainy days are okay.

THE OCTONAUTS

TINK TONK

& the Frown Fish

• MEOMI •

Immedium, Inc. • San Francisco

It was a quiet and rainy afternoon at the bottom of the ocean when...

Professor Inkling was dusting his dust jackets.

Kwazii Kitten was watering his catnip.

Tunip the Vegimal was tossing a salad.

Peso Penguin was pinging...

Tweak Bunny was playing a game.

Captain Barnacles Bear was singing in the rain.

...Shellington Sea Otter was ponging.

Dashi Dog was sounding the Octo-Alert!!!

The crew hurried down to HQ to find Dashi
monitoring the Octopod's screens anxiously.

"There's a fish with a very big frown outside!"
she reported to the others.
"He looks so glum that all the creatures
around him are starting to get upset, too!"

octoBBS 2.1

I DIG CLAMS

```
**** OCTONET BBS V2 ****
LOAD"FROWN FISH",8,1
🐟 ...SMILEY FISH
🐟 ....ANGRY FISH
🐟 ...HUNGRY FISH
🐟 ...SLEEPY FISH
🐟 ....SILLY FISH
??? ....FROWN FISH
?FILE NOT FOUND
■
```

"I can't find a fish like him on the Octonet!"
Dr. Shellington said excitedly.
"Could he be a new species?"

"Octonauts, we should investigate!"
Professor Inkling declared.

Up close, the little fish looked even gloomier.
"Why are you so sad?" Dashi asked with concern.
But the fish only replied, "Glub, glub."

GLUB

GLUB

GLUB

What a dilemma! None of the Octonauts spoke Frownese!

GLUB = SOCK
GLUB = TWO TURNIPS
GLUB GLUB = COOKIE
GLUB =

KNOW your GERMS

"Perhaps if we understood his language, then we could help him," Dr. Shellington proposed.

Shellington and Dashi spent hours in the lab trying to learn Frownese, but it proved to be a very difficult language to translate.

"I don't think we can work much longer," Dashi sighed.
"I'm starting to feel unhappy myself! Let's think of other ways to cheer him up."

"Playing music with my friends always brightens my day," Peso shyly suggested.

He invited everyone to pick up an instrument.

As the crew gathered together to play a happy song, other creatures joined in.

There was a clamcapella group, a sea horchestra, and a baritone whale!

Unfortunately, the Frown Fish didn't have an ear for music and continued to pout.

"It's hard to feel sad when you're being glamorous!"
Kwazii announced with a flourish.
"Let's have a dress-up party!"

The little fish tried on many different costumes...

...but none of them could disguise his sadness.

Dashi held up her favorite camera and asked,
"Why don't we visit the famous Snail Gardens?
We could have a photography field trip!"

SNAIL RAIL

The Octonauts took photos of big snails and little snails, striped snails and polka dot snails.
The Frown Fish, however, wouldn't even smile for the camera.

"A game of miniature golf always tickles my fancy!" revealed Dr. Shellington.
The group putted and swung their way through many aquatic obstacles:
sandshark traps, sea dragons, and electric eel tunnels.

The Frown Fish scored a hole-in-one on the King Crab course but he didn't look any happier.

"I like working with my paws. Let's build something!"
Tweak suggested. Surrounded by gadgets and contraptions,
the crew constructed a robo-tank for the Frown Fish.

Tweak stood back and admired their work, "Now our friend can use his new sea legs to visit us inside the Octopod!"

If possible, the Frown Fish looked even frownier!

Tunip chirped eagerly as it led the group into the kitchen.
"Vegimals love to cook and bake. Maybe the Frown Fish is hungry?"
Dr. Shellington interpreted helpfully.

The whole crew set out to make their favorite pastries.
They baked kelp cakes, kelp muffins, and even a fancy kelp soufflé!

The Frown Fish ate an entire plate of cookies, but he still looked unsatisfied.

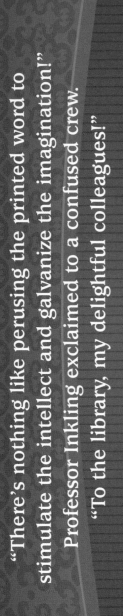

"There's nothing like perusing the printed word to stimulate the intellect and galvanize the imagination!" Professor Inkling exclaimed to a confused crew.

"To the library, my delightful colleagues!"

Professor Inkling read from his favorite book of jokes, but the Frown Fish didn't laugh once. "Frown Fish must not have funny bones," Inkling decided. The other Octonauts weren't too sure... they didn't get the jokes either.

"I always feel better after I exercise!" Captain Barnacles said.
The Octonauts swooshed down the slide,
climbed the jungle gym, and rode the see-saw.

Peso and the Frown Fish sat on the merry-go-round
while Kwazii pushed them faster and faster until...

WHOOOP!

WHOOOP! The Frown Fish flew right off!

The little fish

TURNED...

BOUNCED...

AND ROLLED OVER.

Everyone rushed over in alarm.
They had only been trying to cheer him up,
but now he might have gotten hurt!

To the Octonauts' surprise, the Frown Fish had a BIG smile on his face!

"Of course!" Professor Inkling realized.
"He's not a frown fish... he's an upside-down fish!"

ENCYCLOPEDIA AQUATICA

UPSIDE-DOWN CATFISH
(Synodontis nigriventris)

These whiskered fish like to spend time upside down. They also enjoy music, costume parties, field trips, miniature golf, tinkering, baking, reading and exercising.

(Synodontis nigriventris)

263

"There are different types of fish that swim upside down; it's easier for them to spot food. This chap is a fine example of an Upside-Down Catfish!"

Everyone laughed in relief to discover that
their new friend had been smiling the whole day!
The catfish made a big "ERP!" and turned himself
back upside down... or was it right side up?

THE OCTONAUTS

CAPTAIN BARNACLES BEAR

Captain Barnacles is a brave polar bear extraordinaire and the leader of the Octonauts crew. He's always the first to rush in and help whenever there's a problem. In addition to adventuring, Barnacles enjoys playing his accordion and writing in his captain's log.

PESO PENGUIN

Peso is the medic for the team. He's an expert at bandaging and always carries his medical kit with him in case of emergencies. He's not too fond of scary things, but if a creature is hurt or in danger, Peso can be the bravest Octonaut of all!

TWEAK BUNNY

Tweak is the engineer for the Octonauts. She designed and built the Octopod along with the team's growing fleet of GUPs. Tweak enjoys tinkering and inventing tools that sometimes work in unexpected ways.

SHELLINGTON SEA OTTER

Dr. Shellington is a nerdy sea otter scientist who loves doing field research and working in his lab. He's easily distracted by rare plants and animals, but his knowledge of the ocean is a big help in Octonaut missions.

KWAZII KITTEN

Kwazii is a daredevil orange kitten with a mysterious pirate past. He loves excitement and traveling to exotic places. His favorite hobbies include long baths, racing the GUP-B, and general swashbuckling.

DASHI DOG

Dashi is a smart dachshund who oversees operations in the Octopod HQ and launch bay. She programs the computers and manages all ship traffic. She's also the Octonauts' official photographer and enjoys taking photos of undersea life.

PROFESSOR INKLING OCTOPUS

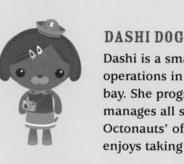

Professor Inkling is a brilliant, Dumbo octopus oceanographer. He founded the Octonauts with the intention of furthering underwater research and preservation. Because of his delicate, big brain, he prefers to help the team from his library in the Octopod.

TUNIP THE VEGIMAL

Tunip is one of many Vegimals, a special sea creature that's part vegetable and part animal. They speak their own language that only Shellington can understand (sometimes!). Vegimals help out around the Octopod and love to bake kelp cakes, kelp cookies, kelp soufflé…